LOST IN THE FUN HOUSE

Written by Jack Harris
Illustrated by John Costanza

A GOLDEN BOOK • NEW YORK
Western Publishing Company, Inc., Racine, Wisconsin 53404

Brrring! The school bell rang at Acme Looniversity. Buster Bunny, Babs Bunny, Plucky Duck, Furrball, Sweetie, and Hamton all ran outside.

"It's time to party—Buster-style," said Buster. "Today's an extra-special day! Our Thrills and Spills Class is sending us on a field trip to the Acme Amusement Park to see the sights, ride the rides, have fun in the fun house…"

"And eat the food!" said Hamton. "That's the kind of assignment I like best!"

The Acme Amusement Park was a great place.
There were a million and one things to do!

"Wheee," yelled Sweetie on the Ferris wheel.

"Meooowww," cried Furrball as he bumped the
bumper cars.

"Yeaaahhh," screamed Plucky on the roller
coaster.

"When do we eat?" whined Hamton on every
ride.

"It doesn't get any better than this!" said
Buster as he led everybody to the fun house.
"It looks weird," said Babs as she peeked inside.
"When do we eat?" whined Hamton.

"We eat when we're finished having fun," Plucky
told Hamton. But Plucky was nervous about
entering the spooky fun house. Then he had an
idea. "Hamton, if you lead the way, you'll be the
first one out and the first one to the snack bar,"
he said.

Carefully Hamton crept into the fun house. It
was dark, and suddenly something large and
strange stood in front of him. "Yipes!" he
screamed. But then he looked again. "It's only
me," Hamton laughed, "in a fun-house mirror."

Hamton hurried down the hall, looking into mirror after mirror until he stopped short.

He had found a mirror that he really liked. His reflection was tall and lean, the best he'd ever seen! "This one looks *exactly like me*," he said.

Soon Buster led the rest of his friends into the
fun house and past the many magical mirrors.
They twisted and turned, wiggled and waved
until they liked what they saw.

Buster said, "I look like a super rabbit!"
Babs said, "I look like a superstar!"
Plucky said, "I look like an eagle!"
Sweetie said, "I look like a sensational singer!"
Furrball said, "I look like a lion!"

Meanwhile, Hamton hurried on through the fun house. Soon, he found himself lost in a maze of mirrors. He went this way and that way and bumped his snout and started to shout, "Help! I'm lost!"

Hamton's friends all heard him hollering for help.

"We have to hunt for Hamton," said Buster.

Plucky Duck looked at himself in the mirror. He felt heroic. "I'll find that pig," he said as he flew off feeling like an American Eagle.

But soon Plucky was also lost in the maze of
mirrors. He flew this way and that way and
bumped his beak and began to bellow, "That's
just dandy! Now there are dozens of dizzy ducks
in the dark!"

"Help," he heard Hamton holler. "I'm getting
hungry."

The rest of the gang heard Hamton hollering
and Plucky Duck bellowing.
"We have to hunt for Hamton and pinpoint
Plucky," said Buster.

Furrball looked at himself in the mirror. He felt brave! "I'll find that hungry Hamton and that dizzy duck," he said as he raced off feeling like a lion.

But soon Furrball found himself lost in the maze of mirrors. He ran this way and that way and tripped on his tail, which caused him to quietly cry.

"Help," he heard Hamton holler. "I need food!"

The remaining friends heard Hamton hollering, Plucky Duck bellowing, and Furrball fussing.

"We have to hunt for Hamton, pinpoint Plucky, and find Furrball," said Buster.

Sweetie looked at herself in the mirror. "I'll find that piggy pig, that funny fowl, and that tomfool tomcat. They can follow my sweet song," she said as she flew off fast.

But soon she found herself lost in the maze of mirrors. She flew this way and that way until she sang herself silly.

"Help," she heard Hamton holler. "I'm starving."

Now Buster and Babs heard Hamton hollering, Plucky Duck bellowing, Furrball fussing, and Sweetie singing.

"Now we have to hunt for Hamton, pinpoint Plucky, find Furrball, and search for Sweetie," said Buster. "We'll have to be the heroes."

"Just like in the movies," said Babs.

Soon they spotted Sweetie.

"I sang too hard," she could only whisper.

"Help," they heard Hamton holler. "I'm famished."

"Now all we have to do is find Furrball, pinpoint Plucky, and hunt for Hamton," said Buster.

The trio trekked through the fun house until they found the flustered Furrball twisting his tail.

"You're safe with us now!" said Babs.

"Meow," said Furrball.

"Help," they heard Hamton holler. "I need supper."

The foursome finally pinpointed Plucky. He was unbending his beak so he could speak. "Just my luck," he clucked, "to be a flexible duck."

"Well, we pinpointed Plucky, successfully sought Sweetie, and found Furrball," said Buster. "Now all we have to do is hunt for Hamton!"

They all listened for Hamton's hollering, but heard nothing! Had something happened to Hamton?

Now the friends were worried about hungry Hamton. They looked this way and that way, but they couldn't find him, or hear him anywhere, here or there.

Finally, the group bumped and bumbled and bonked their way through the maze of mirrors and out of the fun house.

Once outside, they heard, "Hi! What took you so long?"

"It's Hamton," shouted Babs. "He's over there at the snack bar."

"How did you find your way out of the fun house?" Buster asked.

"Oh, it was easy," Hamton said. "When I couldn't yell for help anymore, I decided to focus on the smell of the food and followed it right out of the fun house."

Buster and Babs and Sweetie and Plucky and Furrball all looked at Hamton. They'd been bonked and bruised and baffled and busy all because of Hamton. Now here he was, no longer hungry, and very happy...and they weren't!

The group slowly began to surround Hamton.
Hamton began to back away from them. But just
then, right before they were going to pounce on
the portly pig, they smelled his food. "I'm getting
hungry," said Buster.

"I need food," said Babs.

"I'm starving," said Plucky.

"I'm famished," said Furrball.

"I need supper," said Sweetie.

So they all sat down to a hearty meal.

Full of food and fun, the buddies boarded the
bus back to school. But not before a stop at the
gift shop. They each bought a miniature magical
fun-house mirror.

"These are amazing mirrors," bubbled Babs.
"They make you look any way you can imagine
yourself to be!"

And everyone agreed!